House Party

Eric Walters

orca soundings

Orca Book Publishers

Library and Archives Canada Cataloguing in Publication

Walters, Eric, 1957-

House party / written by Eric Walters.

(Orca soundings)
ISBN 978-1-55143-743-9 (bound)
ISBN 978-1-55143-741-5 (pbk.)

I. Title. II. Series.

PS8595.A598H69 2007   jC813'.54   C2007-903837-9

Summary: Trying desperately to fit in and make friends, Casey and her
friend hold a house party when her parents are out of town.

First published in the United States, 2007
Library of Congress Control Number: 2007930416

Orca Book Publishers gratefully acknowledges the support for its publishing
programs provided by the following agencies: the Government of Canada
through the Book Publishing Industry Development Program and the Canada
Council for the Arts, and the Province of British Columbia through the BC
Arts Council and the Book Publishing Tax Credit.

Cover design: Teresa Bubela
Cover photography: Getty Images

Orca Book Publishers
PO Box 5626, Station B
Victoria, BC Canada
V8R 6S4

Orca Book Publishers
PO Box 468
Custer, WA USA
98240-0468

www.orcabook.com
Printed and bound in Canada.
Printed on 100% PCW recycled paper.

010 09 08 07 • 5 4 3 2 1

To those kids who choose to party responsibly.

Chapter One

There was a knock on the bedroom door.

"Hello, it's me!" my mother called from the hallway.

"Come in!" I called back. I put down my book, and Jen quickly minimized the MSN window on the computer. Her school assignment now filled the screen.

My mother always knocked before she entered. She poked her head in the door and I looked up from where I was lying on my bed, studying math.

"Are you girls studying hard?" she asked.

"As hard as we can," Jen said.

That was only a half-lie. I'd been studying hard because I had a big math test on Monday and math wasn't one of my strengths. Jen, on the other hand, had spent almost all her time on MSN talking to people she didn't know, hadn't met and probably never would meet. If it was possible to be addicted to the Internet, Jen was.

"I was thinking it might be time for you two to take a break," my mother said. "I've just taken some cookies out of the oven."

"I told you I could smell cookies," Jen said.

"Double chocolate with extra chips," my mother said.

"I *love* your cookies," Jen said, and my mother smiled.

Jen wasn't kidding. She did love my mother's cookies. And her pies and cakes and pretty well anything else she baked. Jen liked sweets. A lot. Probably more than was good for her.

Jen had a little bit of a *weight* problem, and she was always on some sort of diet, trying to lose a few pounds. She switched back and forth from diet to diet. Each new one was "guaranteed" to drop the weight.

I knew which method would probably work—don't eat so much and exercise more—but that one hadn't come up yet.

It wasn't that Jen was fat, because she wasn't. She was just a little plump. She was a bit overweight, not more than ten or fifteen pounds for sure.

That wasn't how she saw herself, though. As far as Jen was concerned, she was just plain fat. And worse, those extra pounds were the reason that things didn't work out for her. She was positive she was only a few pounds away from boyfriends, popularity, fame and fortune.

"So, do you want some milk and cookies?" my mother asked.

"A cookie, or *two*, would be great," I said, giving Jen the evil eye. "But could you bring them up here so we could keep studying?"

"I would never want to get in the way of studying," she said, "but there was something I wanted to talk to you about as well."

I felt the hair on the back of my neck go up.

"What do you want to talk about?" I asked, trying not to show my anxiety. I didn't like these sorts of conversations. Six months ago, that had been the first line my parents had used when they told me that we were moving—leaving behind everybody and everything I'd ever known to come down here to live.

"Nothing serious. It can wait until after dinner."

I sat up on the edge of the bed. "It doesn't have to wait. Let's talk now."

"Sure, if you want."

"I want." That was another half-lie. I didn't want to talk about anything really, but I'd rather talk about it now than later.

Talking about it later left too much time for my imagination to play around.

"You know your father is going away on business this weekend, right?"

"Yeah," I said, suspiciously. His business took him back to our old town at least once a month.

"I was thinking that it would be good for me to go along with him. It's easier to take care of the house closing details in person."

Our house had just sold two weeks ago. It had been on the market since we'd moved. In my heart—if not in my head—I figured that if we didn't sell the house we'd eventually just move back home. Now it was gone, along with my last faint hopes.

"So that would mean you have to come with us," she said.

"That would be great!" I exclaimed. I could visit with old friends and...no I couldn't.

"I can't go," I said. "I have a soccer game on Saturday morning and a math exam on Monday."

"You could miss the game, and there's no law that says you can't study there," my mother said.

"First off, I really shouldn't miss the game, and second, while there's no law about me studying there, it wouldn't do much good. I need Jen to help me. Without her, I'm dead."

"I'm sorry, Casey, but I really need to go and we can't leave you on your own."

"She could stay with me!" Jen said.

I turned to my mom. "Could I?"

"I don't see why not," my mom said. "Should you check with your mother?"

Jen shook her head. "She's always good about things like that."

"Just give her a call," my mother said. "It will settle my mind to know that it's all taken care of."

"No problem. I'll just tell her that Casey needs somebody to babysit her. I'll take good care of her."

"You, taking care of me?" I gasped.

Jen had become my best friend since I'd moved here, but she was not the most responsible person in the world. She didn't just need a babysitter. She practically needed a keeper. She was always suggesting something or other that could potentially get us in trouble.

"You know, I could just stay here by myself," I suggested.

"You're too young."

"I'm fifteen, not five," I protested. "I'm old enough to be left alone at home."

"Alone, yes. Overnight, no," my mother said.

"I'd be fine."

"It's easy to say that, but *I* don't even like being at home alone at night," my mother said.

Actually I didn't really like being home by myself when my parents were out for the evening. The house was old and it made serious squeaks and creaks. It sometimes sounded like somebody was walking around when there was nobody here but me.

"I'm *old* enough to be alone, and you *could* leave me alone, but it would be okay for me to stay at Jen's." I paused.

A different solution came to mind. "Or maybe Jen *could* stay here with me."

"Yeah, I could check and see if I could stay here overnight," Jen said. "That would be fun!"

My mother shook her head emphatically. "I don't think so, but please check to make sure it's all right for Casey to sleep at your house."

Chapter Two

I came back to my room carrying a tray holding two glasses of milk and four cookies. Jen was still on the phone with her mother. There was no question that I'd be able to sleep over. Jen's mother never said no to her. Jen said she hadn't heard a "no" from either parent since they had separated the previous year.

"Okay…sure…no problem," Jen said. "I'll be home around seven…okay…thanks."

She put down the phone, looked at me and smiled.

"It's all set. My mother said it was all right for me to sleep here on Saturday night."

"That's good. Then I can...wait a second... did you say for *you* to sleep *here*?"

She nodded.

"That wasn't what you were supposed to ask. I was supposed to sleep at *your* house."

"But that wouldn't be as much fun," she said.

"But my mother said you couldn't sleep here, but that I could sleep at your house."

"And that's why we're not going to tell your mother. Or mine."

"But we can't do that!" I protested.

"Of course we can. I only have two questions," Jen said. "How many and who?"

"What are you talking about?" I demanded.

"Who do we invite, and how many do we invite."

"Invite to what? Invite where?"

She smiled. "To the party, this Saturday, right here at your house."

"But we're not having a party. My parents would never let me have a party."

"That's why we're not inviting them, asking them or telling them," Jen said. "What they don't know, they can't object to."

"I can't do that," I said, shaking my head.

"Why not?"

"My parents would kill me if they found out I was throwing a party while they were gone."

"First off, they wouldn't actually *kill* you. What's the worst thing they could do? Ground you? Take away your allowance?"

"They could do that."

"Big deal. If they took away your allowance, I'd treat you for a couple of weeks. Besides, they're not going to find out. They're going to be hundreds of miles away, right?"

"Yeah."

11

"No matter how loud we turn up the music, they won't be able to hear it from that far away."

"But somebody could tell them," I protested.

"Who?"

"Your mother for one."

"We just keep them away from each other for a few weeks, and by then it'll be done and past."

"How about neighbors?"

"You told me your parents hardly know the neighbors. Besides, do your neighbors usually know what's going on inside your house?"

"Of course not!"

"Then why would this Saturday be any different?" she asked. "Nobody would know if we had a few people over, would they?"

"I guess not."

"Besides, you hardly have neighbors."

She was right about that too. Our street was at the edge of town, and our house was at the end of our street. It dead-ended into a field, and our nearest neighbors were two properties over.

"It takes money to throw a party," I said. "Pop and chips and decorations and—"

"No decorations. This isn't some lame kid's birthday party with balloons. We'll just ask people to bring stuff. Sort of a BYOB. You know—bring your own bottle...of pop...or whatever."

That "whatever" scared me.

"It's Thursday night. Do you really think we can get things organized and get out invitations and get people to come here for Saturday night?"

"That's two nights from now."

"But people probably already have things that they've planned to do," I said, trying to find another reason to defeat the plan.

"Maybe they could just change their plans. You know, the way we'll change our plans and not go to that incredible party that's being thrown by the football team."

"We're invited to a football team party?" I gasped. "I didn't even know they were having a party."

"I don't know either," Jen said.

I felt all confused. "But…but…you said that—"

"Don't listen to what I said. Listen to what I'm going to say. The reason we don't know about a football party is because even if they *were* having a party, do you really think they'd be inviting us?"

I knew what she meant, but I didn't know what to say.

"Have you been going to parties that I don't know about?" Jen asked.

"Of course not!" I protested.

"I haven't been going to them either. We're not invited to the A-list parties. Let's be honest. We're not invited to any parties."

"There was Melissa's birthday party."

"Yeah, and that was pretty exciting. Ten girls in her basement, playing Twister and eating ice-cream cake. Is that your idea of a party?"

I did like the ice-cream cake, but I got the idea.

"To get invited to real parties, parties

with boys and beer, you have to invite people to your house first," she said. "This isn't just about one party at your house. This is about opening a door for other parties—parties that we can go to for the rest of the year."

I used to go to parties. I used to know everybody in the school, in the whole town, and everybody knew me. Here I knew nobody, and nobody knew me.

"Aren't you tired of spending Saturday nights watching *Saturday Night Live* instead of actually *living*?" She paused. "Isn't it time we got a life?"

I had a life, I really did. It just wasn't here.

"Were you lying to your mother when you said you weren't a baby?" she asked.

"I'm no baby."

"You're fifteen. You don't need a babysitter. Come on, Casey, I know you're nervous about all this, but it could work. It really could."

"And lots of things could go wrong."

"Lots could, but we'll make sure nothing

does, and if it does, we'll fix it. We can do this as long as we work together."

"I don't know," I said.

"Casey, this isn't just for you. This is for *me*," she pleaded. "You've only been here a few months. I've been here forever and I'm tired of being on the outside looking in. I want to be *in*."

"You are in," I said. "Lots of kids like you."

"Lots of the *wrong* kids like me. I'm tired of being asked out by kids who play in the school band."

"Hey, I play in the band!"

"And would you go out with any of those guys?"

There were a couple of guys who were cute, and I liked one of the trumpet players... but what was I supposed to say now?

"You know if my mother was going away, I'd throw a party myself and you'd be the first person I'd invite. But my mother never goes away, and if she did, I'd have to stay at my father's." She paused. "So?"

"I don't know."

"You have to admit it would be fun being on our own, right?"

I nodded. It *would* be fun.

"And it doesn't have to be big. Just a few people. What harm would it do to have a few people over?"

I sighed. "How about if we get down to studying?" I asked.

"I'll help with your homework on one condition," she said.

"What's the condition?"

"I want you to just think about this. You don't have to say yes, but don't say no. Just think about it. Okay?"

"I could think about it."

"And just think about it being a small gathering. A few people...maybe eight or ten or so. Not a party...just a small gathering. Would that be okay?"

"I can think about it."

I didn't like any of it. But what harm would there be in thinking about it? And even if I did agree, what would be bad about having a few people over?

Chapter Three

"Now, girls, you're sure you don't want a ride over to Jennifer's house?" my mother asked.

"No, it's better if we study here," Jen said. "It's quieter."

"Especially with you and Dad gone," I said. "We can get more done here."

"And then I'm going to watch Casey's soccer game, and then we'll go over to my house."

"Okay. There's food in the cupboards, leftover meat loaf in the fridge, and here," my mother said. She reached into her pocket and pulled out a twenty-dollar bill. "I want you to order pizza tonight so your mother doesn't have to cook."

Jen reached out and took the money. "Thank you so much, Mrs. Bennett."

"No, thank you. It's nice of you and your mother to have Casey stay with you tonight."

"It's my pleasure," Jen said.

"Maybe I should phone your mother and thank her for letting Casey stay with you."

"No!" Jen said loudly. "Um...my mom isn't home right now...she's out...you know...shopping. But I'll tell her for you."

"You have your key?" my mother asked.

"Yes, I have my key," I said.

"Be sure you lock up when you leave."

"I'll lock up."

"I know you will. It's so good that we know we can trust you."

I had to work hard not to look down at the floor. *Trust* wasn't the word that came to mind. Neither did the word *good*. Instead I was feeling guilty and deceptive.

Not just about what I was doing to my parents, but because, in the back of my mind, I had thought that if anything went really wrong I could always blame Jen. It *was* her fault. She'd made me do it, even when I really didn't want to.

But I knew that wasn't true. I wanted to do this as much as she did. I was tired of being on the outside too. I wanted to be on the inside, the way I'd been before we'd moved.

I knew that no matter what happened, this was just as much my doing as hers. We were in this together, for better or worse.

"You have my cell phone number," my mother said, "and of course you have your nana's number. She was so sad when she heard her favorite granddaughter wasn't coming along."

"I just have too much work to—"

"I explained it all," my mother said.

"We even told her how you were staying home because you wanted to study and how proud we are of you for doing that."

If only they knew.

"Now, no candles. Please be careful with the stove, don't open the door to strangers, don't—"

"Don't play with matches, run with scissors or eat anything that you find on the ground," I said, cutting her off.

"Unless it's just fallen on the ground," Jen said. "You know, the five-second rule for fallen food."

"Okay, okay, I get it," my mother said.

There was a faint honking of a car horn. My father. He'd already said his good-byes and was waiting, not so patiently, in the car.

"I better get going," my mother said. She hugged Jen, and then she wrapped her arms around me.

"Be smart, be safe," she whispered in my ear. She always said that. She had since I was little enough to remember. Usually I listened. This weekend I knew I

21

wasn't going to be smart. I just hoped I'd be safe.

We followed her to the door as my father honked again. I leaned out the door and waved, and my father smiled and waved back as my mother got into the car. We stood there waving and watched as they drove away, turning the corner and disappearing.

"I guess we should get going," Jen said. "We have no time to waste."

"I guess you're right. We better study, and then I've got to get to soccer and—"

"There's no time for soccer or for studying. We have to get things ready for the party."

"But I can't miss my game."

"Sure you can. It's only a house-league game. We have too many things to do."

"What sort of things?"

"For starters, we have to put things out and put things away."

I gave her a confused look.

"We have to put out cups and plates, and we have to put away anything that's breakable or valuable. Things like all those figurines your mother has in the living room."

"I hadn't even thought of that," I said.

"Always thinking," Jen said, tapping herself on the side of the head. "But before we do that, we have to take care of the most important thing you need for a party...people."

"But we already invited people...last night and yesterday at school."

"We invited *some* people."

"We invited fifteen people and that's all we're going to invite," I said firmly. "That's what we agreed to, a small gathering."

"We agreed to *have* fifteen people," Jen said. "Do you really think that everybody we invited is going to come?"

"Well..."

"You're the one who said we weren't giving people much notice. For a party to work we need to have fifteen or twenty—"

"We agreed fifteen," I said, cutting her off.

"Fifteen plus us."

"Okay, seventeen, but not twenty."

"Sure, seventeen, not fifteen, but not *five*."

"We invited fifteen."

"But what if only five show up?" Jen asked. "It wouldn't be a party. It would be a *disaster*."

I pictured seven people sitting around in my living room. There would be nobody talking, nobody dancing, just people staring at each other.

"We would be the laughingstock of the whole school. We'd be the girls who threw a party and nobody came."

"That would be awful."

"That would be worse than awful. We'd have to change schools!"

Jen could be a drama queen sometimes.

"I figure we have to invite a few extra people to make sure we have enough people to make it a party."

"But what if we invite more people and they all show up?" I questioned.

"First off, they we

prepare the house so tha

damaged, and third, what

between fifteen and twenty

"Ten."

"Funny. Whether it's fifteen   .wenty-
five, it's a party. If we only have five, it's
a disaster. Isn't it better to aim high?"

"I guess," I reluctantly admitted.

"Besides, do you think your parents
would see any difference between fifteen
and twenty-five?" Jen asked.

"Is that supposed to be reassuring?"

"No, just a reality check. Would they
be any madder if you had a few more
people?"

I shook my head.

"Even if you didn't have a party, they'd
be just as mad because you didn't stay at
my house."

"We could still stay at your house
tonight," I said.

"No, we can't. How would I explain that
to my mother?"

I didn't have an answer. "I guess that

y, party or no party, if they found
d be just as dead."

"Then what you're saying is you have nothing to lose," Jen said. "So why not go for it?"

Chapter Four

I wrapped up the last figurine with toilet paper and carefully put it in the box beside the others. I was taking Jen's advice to heart. I was going to make sure there wasn't much left for anybody to break. It was starting to look like we'd just moved in.

Actually, I was putting things back in the same boxes we'd used to move with. The boxes had been unpacked and put into the crawl space under the stairs. Now they'd been repacked and put back down there. I just wanted to be safe. Better safe than sorry. Then again, if I really wanted safe, we wouldn't be throwing this party to begin with.

I knew part of the reason I wanted to have the party. I was fifteen—which meant I was almost sixteen—and I wasn't a baby anymore. They didn't trust me to be home alone for a night by myself. How fair was that? By next year I could live on my own if I wanted. I could sleep alone—at least with Jen here—have a party, a small gathering, and take care of everything including myself. This wasn't just a party. This was a declaration of independence.

With Jen upstairs, I'd had a lot of time to think about things like that. Maybe more time than was wise.

I'd also thought things through and was thinking that maybe we shouldn't have the party. The problem was that now that we'd invited people, I didn't know how to *un-throw* it. Besides, I couldn't let my parents be right, even if they'd never know they were wrong.

"Wow."

I turned around. Jen was standing behind me.

"You've really cleaned the place out, " she said.

"I've tried."

It wasn't just the figures, but vases and ornaments. I'd even moved two glass-topped coffee tables into the basement and removed the lights that sat on them.

"I figure if it isn't out, it can't be broken." I paused. "Do you think anything will get broken?"

"I'm not with the psychic hotline, but what's left to get broken?"

I looked around. There was still lots of stuff in the room but nothing that could really be broken. It wasn't like somebody was going to break the piano.

"I guess you're right. How did things go for you?" I asked.

"I invited a few more people."

"Just a few, right?"

"Of course."

"You were up there a long time," I said suspiciously.

"Mostly I was just lurking around on MSN, trying to see if I could figure out if anybody was talking about coming here tonight."

"And?"

She shook her head. "Not a word."

Instantly I went from thinking that we shouldn't throw a party and worrying about there being too many people, to feeling worried that there wouldn't be enough people.

I looked around the room. It was a big, semi-empty room in a big house. It could hold a whole lot of people. And the more I cleared away, the more people it *could* hold.

"We could invite a few more," I said.

"That would be smart," Jen said. "Nothing says loser more than throwing a party and having nobody come. That would be awful for you."

"For *me*? Don't you mean for *us*?"

"It wouldn't be good for me, but it's not like it's *my* house."

I was going to argue, but she was right. It was my house, and I was the one with the most to lose if this didn't go right.

"Well, do we invite more people?" she asked.

"My grandmother used to say *In for a penny, in for a pound*," I said.

"And that means?"

"It means that we invite some more people."

Jen smiled. "I think your grandmother is one smart lady."

"I don't think any of this has anything to do with being smart," I said.

"Okay, maybe smart isn't the right word. So you're okay with us inviting more people, right? I don't want to do anything you don't want me to do. It *is* your house."

I didn't answer right away. Maybe it wasn't too late to be smart and call the whole thing off.

"Well?" Jen asked.

"I don't know. I'm just worried."

"Sometimes, when I'm worried about something happening, I try to imagine what would be the very, very *worst* thing that could happen," Jen said.

"And that's supposed to make me feel better?"

"It does. Think about it. What's the worst thing that could happen?"

"I don't know. I guess that something gets broken," I said.

"You've pretty well taken care of that."

She was right. I had done a pretty good job of putting everything away.

"Somebody could spill something on the carpet," I said.

"Or *throw up* on the carpet," Jen added.

"That would be worse."

"But either way we'd just clean it up. Anything else?"

"My parents finding out would be pretty bad."

"You're right, but whether it's fifteen people or twenty-five, they're going to be just as mad, so there's nothing worse about it being slightly bigger." She paused. "So?"

"So we invite some more people."

"Yes, sir!" Jen said. She first saluted me, and then she disappeared up the stairs.

I took a deep breath. This was starting to feel like it was spinning faster and faster. It almost felt like I was climbing onto a roller coaster. There's that moment when they strap you in, when you know you're going on a ride, and you really don't know how much fun or how scary it's going to be, but you have no choice. You're going. Some people loved roller coasters. I didn't.

Chapter Five

I sat staring at the clock. The house was
so quiet that I could hear the clock ticking
from clear across the room. That seemed
right. Time was everything now. We had
one hour to go before the start of the
party—it was almost eight o'clock. Part of
me couldn't wait for it all to begin, to see
how it was going to work out. The other part
of me was just dreading the whole thing. I
didn't want nine o'clock to arrive. I wanted
time to stand still.

"How do I look?" Jen asked as she entered the room.

I looked her up and down carefully. I knew she wanted a serious answer. I also knew that whatever answer I gave, it probably wouldn't make her happy.

She was wearing jeans—designer, expensive and tight...maybe a little too tight. Her top was low cut, but not too low cut. Her hair was all done up—she'd been working on it for the last hour—and she was wearing brand-new earrings that dangled down.

"You look good," I said.

"Only good? I was hoping for great."

"I meant to say great!" I stammered.

":Now you're just lying. I wish I knew about this two weeks ago. I would have started dieting. Do I look fat in these jeans?" she demanded as she turned around.

"You don't look fat in *any* jeans. You aren't fat."

"I am compared to Sarah Jenkins."

"Compared to Sarah Jenkins, a toothpick is fat."

Jen chuckled. "Maybe you're right, but don't mention that to her tonight."

"Sarah Jenkins is coming to our party?" I asked.

"I invited her."

"I think we've only exchanged a few words, and she wasn't very nice to me when we did. But maybe it's just that I don't know her," I said.

"Believe me, if you get to know her you'll find out she's *really, really* not nice at all."

"Then why did you invite her?" I asked.

"You want a good party, you have to invite the right people, and, nice or not, she's one of the right people," Jen said matter-of-factly.

"Maybe she won't even show."

"We'll find out soon enough. We better take care of the last details. Do you have something like a big pot that we can use as a punch bowl?"

"We have an actual punch bowl," I said.

"Fantastic. Do you have some frozen juices?"

"Yeah, in the freezer downstairs."

"Good. I'll get the juices and you get the punch bowl."

I went upstairs while Jen went downstairs. The punch bowl was in the hall cupboard. I pulled down the box, brought it to the kitchen and carefully removed the punch bowl from the box.

It was heavy. It was made of crystal. There was a ladle and a dozen little crystal glasses. I picked up one of the glasses and looked at it. I remembered the bowl and glasses from when I was a little kid. I loved the way the light sparkled as it passed through the glasses. We only used them for special family gatherings. They had belonged to my great-grandmother.

Maybe this wasn't so smart. I'd already put things away so they wouldn't be broken, and here I was putting out something that was valuable.

"That's beautiful," Jen said. She was holding a bunch of cans of frozen juice in her arms.

"It is, but I'm just worried about somebody

dropping a cup and breaking it or one of them getting lost."

"Forget the cups. Put them away and we'll use the plastic cups."

That made perfect sense. I put the glasses back in the box and closed the lid. It was all right to use the punch bowl. What could happen to a punch bowl? Besides, we always used it for special occasions, and this party was a pretty special event.

"You want to help me with these?" Jen said as she dumped the juices on the counter.

"Sure." I opened the drawer and pulled out an opener.

There was a can of grape juice, two orange, a peach and two cranberry juices.

As I opened them, Jen dumped them into the punch bowl.

"This is a lot of juice," I said.

"People get thirsty." Jen shrugged.

"I'm just worried my mother might notice them missing."

"So what?" Jen said. "Tell her you made some juice. It isn't like she caught you stealing their booze. Come to think of it, where do your parents keep their booze?"

"Don't worry about that. I've got it all packed away."

"I'm not worried. I just need some of it for the punch."

"You're going to spike the punch?" I gasped.

"It would be a pretty lame party without some alcohol, don't you think?" Jen asked.

"But we can't do that. My father will notice for sure if I take all his alcohol!"

"Nobody's talking about *all*. Just a little. I want to put in just enough that people can taste it, so we can *say* that the punch is spiked. I only need a few ounces. Do you think he'll miss a few ounces?"

I shook my head. He probably wouldn't.

"Vodka would be the best, but we could put in an ounce or two of two or three different types. It's not like anybody is going to be able to tell the difference.

We'll put in so little that somebody would have to drink the whole punch bowl to get a buzz."

I guessed that was smart. Jen had been really thinking this thing through.

"I'll get the booze while you start making the punch, " I said.

I'd taken the bottles out of the cabinet in the living room and had stored them, along with everything else, under the stairs. I opened up the flaps on two or three boxes before I found the right one. I dragged it out of the storage locker and put it on the little buffet in the basement.

There weren't that many bottles inside. My parents weren't what you would call "drinkers." My mother mainly had a little white wine with supper, and I'd hardly ever seen my father have anything to drink except an occasional beer when he was cutting the grass.

I pulled out a big bottle of vodka, a second one of gin and a third of whiskey. All three bottles were almost full. I carried them upstairs to the kitchen.

Jen had already finished opening all the little cans and dumping them into the punch bowl. She was now adding water to the colorful frozen mess. I put the bottles down beside the punch bowl.

"This is going to taste really good," Jen said as she dumped in a pitcher of water.

I grabbed a wooden spoon and started to stir up the mixture.

Jen picked up the vodka bottle and unscrewed the cap. She sloshed some into the punch bowl.

"Be careful!" I warned. "Not too much!"

"Of course not." She stopped and put the lid back on the bottle.

It looked to be not much different than the level before she started pouring. She did the same with the other two bottles. I kept stirring the whole concoction, the spoon clinking against the sides of the bowl.

"Time for a sample," Jen said.

She dipped in a plastic cup and scooped out a little bit. She sipped it.

"Well?"

She handed me the cup. "See for yourself."

I took a sip. "It's good, very good!"

"I think so. Can you taste the alcohol?"

I took another sip. "Maybe just a little."

"Then it's perfect. By the way, we shouldn't drink anything else tonight. We have to keep track of everything, so we can't afford for this to be a party where we get drunk."

"I've never gotten drunk!" I said.

"Never?"

"Never," I said. "Have you?"

She shook her head.

"By the way," Jen said, "are you going to wear that top?"

"What's wrong with this top?"

"Nothing...I was just wondering, that's all," she said.

"I *was* going to wear it." That was now out of the question. I went upstairs to change.

Chapter Six

"Well," Jen said, "it's almost official. We've moved from nobodies to big losers. We're the ones who gave a party and nobody came."

"It's still early," I said, trying to be reassuring.

"It's ten after nine. Ten minutes after people were supposed to arrive, and do you see any people?" She gestured around the room.

"Do you know what tonight is?" Jen asked.

"A bad night for giving a party?"

"It's a bad night to be alive!" she screamed. "I thought somebody would show up, but it's just you and me. It's not like we didn't invite people, because we did!"

She looked like she was going to start crying.

"It's okay," I said. "It's probably because there wasn't enough notice. The next time my parents go away, we'll know a lot sooner and we can start planning and inviting people sooner."

"That would just make it worse! That would give them even more time to ignore us. This is proof positive that you and I are two—"

The doorbell rang, cutting her off.

"The doorbell," I said. I had an amazing ability to point out the obvious. It rang again.

"You get it!" Jen ordered. "I have to check my makeup!"

As she ran from the room, she reached over and cranked the volume up on the stereo. Music filled the room.

The doorbell rang again. I raced for the door. My heart was pounding. I reached the door as the bell rang again. This was bizarre. I was feeling excited and scared to answer my own front door. I took a deep breath, and then I threw it open.

There were four boys standing there. I didn't know any of them. I wasn't surprised because Jen did most of the inviting and knew most of the people.

"Is this the place where the party's taking place?" one of them asked.

"This is it," I said. "I'm Casey. This is my house."

"Hey, Casey. I'm Mike and this is Steve, Mo and Malik."

"Come in," I said and gestured for them to enter. "It's still early, so not many people have arrived yet," I tried to explain.

"Nothing wrong with being early," one of them said.

"Yeah, that's cool."

"Jen's upstairs."

"Cool."

"And there's punch in the kitchen...it's in a bowl...and there's alcohol...we put alcohol in it...vodka and whiskey and gin," I stammered. "So help yourself."

"I think we've already taken care of that part," one of them said—I think it was Mo, but I really couldn't keep track of all the names.

He opened up his coat, reached inside a pocket and pulled out a bottle. It was like a magic trick as this gigantic bottle of vodka just appeared.

"Plus we have beer," one of the others said.

He pulled off a backpack, and I heard bottles clinking together.

"There are plastic cups in the kitchen by the punch bowl. Just help yourselves."

"We will, thanks for having us," Mike said.

"Thanks for coming and—"

The doorbell rang again, cutting me off.

"You better get that," Mike said.

They went upstairs, and I went to grab the door. Two guys and a girl walked in. I didn't know the guys but I knew the girl—Ashley from my law class.

"Hey, Casey," Ashley said. "These are my friends, Brian and Ryan. They're such good friends they even rhyme."

They nodded at me, and I nodded back.

"There's punch upstairs," I said, "but be careful. It's spiked with alcohol."

"I'm going to stick with wine," Ashley said. She pulled a bottle out from under her jacket.

"Fancy-looking bottle," Brian said. "But look, it's got a cork. Why didn't you get something with a screw cap?"

"My father doesn't buy wine with screw caps," she said. "He only buys the good stuff."

"Your father bought that for you?" I gasped.

They laughed and I realized that was a pretty dumb question.

"This isn't like a bush party," Ashley said. "I'm sure that Casey has a corkscrew."

"Of course. Up in the kitchen. The drawer just to the right of the fridge."

Brian and Ryan headed up the stairs. Ashley started after them, stopped and turned around.

"Thanks for hosting the party," Ashley said.

"Thanks for coming…it didn't take much effort."

"It's just that it's pretty brave of you to do, that's all."

"Brave? What do you mean?" I asked.

"Ashley!" Ryan bellowed from the kitchen. "You're slowing down our drinking time! Come on!"

"I'm coming!" she yelled back. "Talk to you later."

I guess she must have meant it was brave because my parents would kill me if they found out. They actually wouldn't kill me. I'd be grounded, but if that happened it happened. Sometimes you had to be prepared to pay the price to get what you wanted.

There was a pounding on the door. Startled, I almost screamed. I recovered and scrambled over to the door. It was four—no, five people. Three girls and two guys. I recognized them from around school, but they were a couple of grades ahead of me.

"Is this the party place?" one of the guys asked.

"Yes, I'm Casey and this is the place where—"

"Yahoooo!" one of the guys screamed. They burst through the door and brushed past me. There were no introductions. They just moved upstairs. I guess there'd be time to get to know who they were later. I was sure Jen would introduce me.

I did a quick count—four, then three and now five, plus Jen and me. That was fourteen. No matter what happened now, even if nobody else came, we had ourselves a real party. No one could accuse us of having a party and nobody showing up.

Chapter Seven

The music surged even louder as somebody cranked the stereo up another notch. I didn't know our sound system could go that loud.

I'd stopped trying to count. There had to be at least twenty-five people here. It was amazing to have all the people we invited come on such short notice. I knew Jen had to be thrilled. She certainly looked happy. She was practically beaming. She was buzzing around, talking to people, dancing, laughing and having a great time.

The song ended and Jen gave the boy she was dancing with a hug. Then she came into the kitchen.

"Great party!" she said.

"Not bad," I admitted.

Jen dipped a cup into the punch bowl. She downed the whole cup in one gulp and then refilled it again.

"You should go slow on that stuff," I warned her.

"I'm burning at least as much calories as this on the dance floor."

"It's not the calories I'm worried about. Remember the alcohol?"

"Come on, Casey, you know how little there is in here. I could drink the whole punch bowl and still drive a car."

"You're only fifteen. You don't have a license."

"But if I *did*, this stuff wouldn't affect me. I'm hot and it's good."

"It's not bad," I agreed. I'd had two cups myself.

"Just be careful. You wouldn't want to get drunk," she chided me.

"Funny."

I dipped my cup into the punch bowl. Jen wasn't the only one who was hot and thirsty. It was amazing how all the bodies in the house heated the place up. That and the dancing I'd been doing.

Actually, it was looking like Jen and I were the only ones who were drinking the punch. The bowl was still almost full.

There was a tap on my shoulder and I turned around. It was Mike.

"Do you want to dance?" he asked.

"To this?" I asked. The music was a pounding rap song.

He looked hurt. I wasn't turning him down. It was the song.

"We could try to dance," I said quickly.

He smiled, took me by the hand and led me toward the dance floor—the dining room. There were two other couples on the floor. They looked really awkward trying to dance to rap. At least we wouldn't be the only ones who looked stupid.

We walked into the center of the floor and started dancing. It *was* really awkward.

The music suddenly stopped and another song came on—a slow dance song.

"Is that better?" Mike asked.

"Much better."

He slipped his arms around me and we began dancing. Instantly other couples reacted to the song and rushed into the dining room. We were pushed into the center by the crush of people on all sides and we continued to shuffle to the music.

"Quite a crowd!" Mike said into my ear.

"It is."

"You throw a great party!"

"Thanks."

It *was* a great party. Everywhere there were people dancing, and laughing and talking and drinking. There was a whole lot of drinking going on, but nobody seemed to be drunk...just happy.

Jen suddenly popped her head into the dining room and motioned for me.

Eric Walters

"Can you excuse me," I said to Mike. "Always things to do when you're the host."

"Thanks for the dance."

"Maybe we could dance later on," I suggested.

"For sure."

I squeezed my way through the couples and off the dance floor.

Jen looked worried. "What's happened?" I asked.

"Where can I get a pail and a mop?" she said.

"What happened?" I asked anxiously.

"Nothing serious. A bottle of wine got knocked over."

"I'll get the bucket...where did it get spilled?"

"Downstairs in the rec room."

"On the carpet?"

"Yeah, but it's not bad and it sort of blends in with the brown of the carpet."

I grabbed a roll of paper towels off the kitchen counter and handed it to Jen. "You start blotting it up, and I'll get the bucket and water."

Jen rushed off and I went to the laundry room and grabbed a pail. I squeezed in some soap and filled it up with water. I grabbed a couple of rags that were hanging behind the door.

The pail was heavy, and it bumped against my leg as I moved along the hall and down the stairs, sloshing water onto the floor. Water wasn't bad. Wine was.

Jen was on her knees, blotting up the wine. She was right. It had blended in, and I could hardly see where it had been spilled. I took a rag and soaked the spot with water.

"I told you it wasn't that bad," Jen said.

"Nothing serious," I agreed.

"If this is the worst thing that happens, it'll be one successful party."

"It *is* working well," I said. "There are a lot of people, though."

"Yeah, isn't it great?" Jen shouted.

"I guess so."

Jen started giggling. Her eyes looked all glazed.

"Jen, have you been drinking?"

She giggled even more. "Nothing except the punch, like we agreed. I'm just happy that it's all working out so well. Isn't it a great party?" she yelled.

"Just as great as when you said it a minute ago."

"Oh, yeah, that's right," she said and giggled some more.

"How many people do you think there are?" I asked.

Jen shook her head. "I don't know…a lot… but most of them are people you invited."

"Me? I hardly invited anybody."

"That doesn't make sense. I didn't invite most of them…I don't even *know* most of them," she said, sounding defensive.

"You don't?"

"I thought some of them had to be your friends. That you'd invited them."

"I hardly know anybody here. But if you didn't invite them, and I didn't invite them, how did they know about the party tonight?"

"I guess they just sort of heard through

the grapevine…you know, on MSN or text messaging or something like that," Jen said. "But they all seem like pretty good people."

"I guess so. It seems to be going pretty well."

A big cheer filled the air.

"Let's go and see what's happening," I said to Jen.

We rushed upstairs. There was a crowd of people standing around watching four guys chugging bottles of beer. They were racing to see who could finish their bottle first.

People continued to cheer as the drinkers got closer and closer to the bottom. Two of the guys finished, and then they turned their bottles upside down to show they were empty. The crowd cheered even louder. The bottles weren't completely empty though, and some beer, mostly foam, dripped out and onto the carpet.

I ran over with my pail and rags. Before I could even get there, the crowd surged forward, slapping the two guys on the back and grinding the foam into the carpet. There was no point in even trying to clean it up now.

"Just go with the flow," Jen said. "I saw a carpet cleaner in the storage locker downstairs. Do you know how to use it?"

"Of course I do."

"Good. After it's all over we can just clean the whole carpet. All the carpets."

That made perfect sense. I was sure there'd be little stains all over, not to mention mud and dirt that had been tracked in…it wasn't like people had been leaving their shoes at the door.

"The only bad thing about cleaning the carpets is that the place might be too clean," Jen said.

"How can being too clean be a problem?"

"If it's too clean, your parents will get suspicious—unless you normally clean the carpets when they're not looking."

"No, but I guess we'll have to take that chance," I said.

"Speaking of chances. Why don't you

go and find that cute guy you were dancing with. Just enjoy yourself!"

"I'll try." It would be a whole lot easier if it wasn't my house, or if my house wasn't filled with so many people. People I didn't know. People that Jen didn't know.

Just then the doorbell rang. I ran down to answer it. It was a pizza delivery guy holding a stack of boxes. I opened the door and he stepped in.

"Sorry it took so long," he said.

"So long? But...but I didn't order any pizza," I stammered.

"Is this Forty Calico?"

"Yes."

"I've got ten pizzas. That'll be one hundred and twenty-seven bucks." He tried to hand them to me. I backed away.

"I didn't order them, and I don't have that sort of money!"

"Somebody ordered them and somebody better pay!"

"But...but..."

"Hey, pizza!" a guy yelled. A bunch of people rushed toward the delivery guy.

"Nobody gets pizza until I get paid!" he yelled. He was big, and he didn't look like he could be pushed around.

"How much?" a boy in a baseball cap asked. I think his name was John.

"A hundred and twenty-seven dollars."

"Hold on." John took off his baseball cap and started moving through the crowd. Some of the people dropped change into the hat, but others put in bills. He went through the living room, into the dining room and disappeared into the kitchen.

"Sorry," I said to the pizza guy. "It won't be long."

"I can wait. Quite the party."

"Thanks."

"Biggest one I've been to tonight."

I wasn't sure if that was something I was particularly happy about.

John returned. He started counting out the money. It looked like a lot, but was it enough?

"One hundred and nineteen dollars," he said proudly.

"That leaves you eight dollars short," the delivery guy said.

"Hold on. I'll get the rest, " said John.

"Don't bother," I said. I reached into my pocket and pulled out the twenty my mother had given Jen. She had told us it was for pizza. I handed it to the delivery guy.

"And keep the change."

Chapter Eight

I dipped my cup into the punch bowl and filled it up. I took a sip. It tasted a little bitter. Maybe the juice was starting to turn. It didn't matter. I was thirsty. I chugged back the whole glass.

There were people everywhere, in every room. There were even some out front on the grass and in the backyard.

"Hey, nobody is allowed up there!" I yelled at a girl and guy on the stairs. They couldn't hear me over the music and kept going. I ran over to the bottom of the stairs and yelled at them again.

They stopped and looked at me.

"There's nothing up there but bedrooms," I said.

"That's what we're looking for," the girl said. The boy laughed. They started back up the stairs.

"No!" I yelled. "You can't go up there!"

"You can't tell us what to do," the girl said.

"It's my party and my house," I said, trying to sound firm.

"Well, unless you're my mother, you can't tell me and my boyfriend what to do, so just butt out!"

They turned and walked up the stairs. I stood there, stunned. This wasn't right. They couldn't use my parents' room. They couldn't use my room.

I started up after them. Somebody grabbed my arm. It was a guy I didn't know.

"This is your house, right?"

I nodded.

"Good. What's the address here?"

"Um...Forty Calico Court."

"Thanks."

He turned around and put a phone to his ear. Over the music I heard him yell out my address.

"What are you doing?" I asked.

"Just telling a few friends where the party is. Giving them the address."

"But there are too many people here already!" I yelled.

"There can never be too many people! You know how to throw one great party!"

He darted off through the crowd before I could say another word.

Just then the front door opened and more people came in. There were four, five—no, six of them. I didn't recognize any of them.

This was getting really crazy. There was a couple upstairs in one of the bedrooms, and some kid I didn't know was inviting other kids I didn't know to come over, and more and more strangers were just walking into my house. I had to do something. I had to find Jen, and together we had to do something.

I pushed my way into the kitchen, looking for Jen. My eyes widened in shock. There was a girl standing over the punch bowl. She had a bottle of vodka in her hand, and she was pouring it into the punch!

I ran across the room. "What are you doing?" I screamed as I grabbed her arm.

She glared at me. "Careful!" she yelled. "You almost made me spill it!"

"You can't do that!"

"I'm just adding some punch to the punch," she said. "It was pretty weak until we started adding some muscle."

"We? Have other people added things before?" I questioned.

"All night. I noticed you've been enjoying it."

All night. That explained why Jen was acting the way she was. She *was* drunk.

But I'd had five or six glasses myself…My stomach didn't feel the best. I had just thought it was the party and the excitement and everything.

She emptied the rest of the bottle into the punch. Then she took the ladle and mixed it all up. I had to find Jen.

I squeezed out of the room. She wasn't in the dining room on the dance floor, but there had to be ten couples out there now. I threaded my way between the people standing around in the hall—who were these people and how could there be so many of them? I hardly recognized anybody. Then I saw Ashley.

"Ashley, have you seen Jen?"

"Yeah, she's downstairs in the washroom. She wasn't looking so good."

"What do you mean?"

"I think she had too much to drink. She looked like she was going to upchuck."

The punch! She'd been drinking more of it than me.

I went downstairs. There were dozens of people in the room. The TV was on and a music video was blaring. People were talking, laughing, drinking and eating pizza. There was a piece of pizza lying upside down on the carpet. I picked it up, putting it down on the table.

The door to the bathroom was slightly open. I peeked inside.

Jen was on her knees on the floor in front of the toilet. There was a girl standing over her, holding back her hair.

"Jen, I need you to help me!" I yelled. "Things are getting out of control and—"

She bent forward, her whole body convulsed and she threw up into the toilet.

The girl leaned away but kept her hold on Jen's hair, keeping it out of the vomit.

Jen coughed and spit into the toilet. Then she looked up at me.

"It must be the flu. I didn't have anything to drink...just the punch...honest," she said.

"The punch has been spiked! It's almost pure alcohol!"

"That would explain it." She turned back to the toilet and threw up again. It was nothing but liquid, the same color as the punch.

She turned back around. "That feels better," she said, her voice quivering.

"There are too many people in the house," I practically screamed. "And there's going to be more. There was a guy who called his friends and invited them to come over too!"

"Is this your house?" the girl holding Jen's hair asked.

"Yes, it's my place."

"I didn't know who lived here. I got a text message telling me it was an open house with no parents. My friend Bailey told me she read about it in a chat room."

"I didn't tell anybody in a chat room," Jen said.

"Probably somebody you told went into the chat room and told everybody else," the girl said. "There's no telling how many people know about it. It's still early."

"No more people can come!" I screamed. "We have to stop people from coming in!"

Jen unsteadily rose to her feet.

House Party

"You lock the back door," Jen said. "I'll go to the front door and stop people from coming in."

"Do you think you can do that?"

"I'm okay, and if anybody bothers me, I'll puke on them." She gave a weak smile. "Meet me at the front when you're done with the back."

I raced upstairs. The key to the back door was hanging in the hall cupboard. It was a dead bolt, and once it was locked there was no way anybody could get in or out without the key. I ripped the key off the hook and ran to the door. It was wide open, and people were going in and out.

"Excuse me," I said as I pushed my way past some people. "I have to lock up the door and—hey, that's my father's camera!"

A boy I didn't know had my father's camera in his hands. Without even thinking, I grabbed it from him. He didn't fight me. He hardly reacted at all.

"Get out and don't come back!"

"Screw you!" he yelled, but then he walked out the door.

I slammed it shut and locked the door. Nobody was going to be coming in this way at least. Now we just had to control the front door, stop anybody else from walking in, and as soon as somebody left, not let them back inside.

Jen was standing at the front door. Along with her were Mike and Mo.

"They're going to work the door for us," Jen said.

"Thank you so much!" I had to fight the urge to wrap my arms around both of them.

"They'll make sure the door is kept locked and that nobody else gets in," Jen said. "By the way, why do you have a camera with you? Are you taking pictures?"

I looked down at the camera. I'd forgotten I was even carrying it.

"No, no...I caught somebody trying to steal it. I took it away from some guy!"

"That's awful."

Mike put a hand on my shoulder. "We'll try to make sure nobody takes anything out that isn't theirs."

This time I did wrap my arms around him. I felt like I was going to cry, but I forced myself to hold back.

"It's okay. We'll help," Mike said. "Is there anything else we can do?"

"There are people upstairs in the bedrooms. They shouldn't be there."

"I'll go with you and we can take care of that," Jen said.

We started up the stairs. Jen looked a little unsteady. She couldn't have been feeling very well, but she was being a trooper.

She flung open the door to my bedroom and flipped on the light. There were those two kids lying on my bed. The girl screamed and they jumped to their feet.

"What do you think you're doing?" the guy demanded.

"What do you think *you're* doing?" Jen yelled back. "This isn't your house, and you were told not to come up here, so now you have to get out!"

"You can't tell me—"

"Get out now or we call the police!"

He looked like he was going to say something, but he didn't.

"Come on, let's get out of this place!" the girl huffed. She grabbed her shoes from the floor and stomped out of the room, straightening her clothes as she walked.

"Thanks a lot," the guy said. He started out of the room, and then he turned around, grabbed the lamp off my dresser and tossed it against the wall. It shattered into a thousand pieces.

I stood there, speechless. I didn't know what to say.

"I'll check out your parents' room and kick out anybody who's there. Then we'll make sure that nobody else comes upstairs."

"Maybe we should make everybody leave."

Jen shook her head. "I don't think we could do that even if we tried. It might just make things worse. It's almost midnight. People are going to start leaving on their own soon anyway."

She smiled. "Still, it is a pretty good party, don't you think?"

Chapter Nine

I wandered from room to room. I was trying to get a count of how many people there were in the house. There had to be close to a hundred kids. Thank goodness nobody else was going to get inside. Mike and Mo were working the door like a couple of bouncers, letting people out but not letting anybody else in.

There were, of course, some people that I knew, and some who went to our school—but most of them were complete strangers. Even worse, some of them were a lot older than me. They were adults—or at least no longer in high school.

I sidled around the dance floor. It was still crowded, and the music was still so loud that I could hardly hear myself think. Every seat in the living room was taken, and people were standing around talking, laughing. They did look like they were having a good time. I wished I could have been laughing or dancing or talking instead of worrying, cleaning and hoping that it would all end without anything more happening.

There were drinks everywhere. Bottles of beer and little wine coolers, glasses filled with punch or whatever. Along with them were plates—our good plates—lying here and there with crusts of pizza. Somebody had taken down the plates when the pizza had arrived. I kept on gathering up the plates, putting them safely in the laundry room sink, as well as picking up the empty bottles and cups. I was quickly becoming the cleaning staff at my own party.

The most bizarre thought kept rolling around in my head. Despite it all, it really did look like a good party. There was going to be a lot of cleaning up to do, and I hoped my parents wouldn't find out about it, but it just might all work out. Jen and I were throwing a grade-A, top-of-the-line party.

There was the sound of squealing tires and I glanced out the front window. I was stunned by what I saw. I knew people were outside, but I'd had no idea how many. There had to be two hundred kids on our front lawn and the street! Everywhere I looked there were people! I stared, unable to believe the scene. They were standing around in groups, sitting on the curb, lying on my lawn, or sitting on the hoods or trunks of cars. There seemed to be as many cars as there were people. It was like a parking lot, with cars clogging the entire street.

Another car tore away, leaving behind a patch of rubber, and the crowd cheered its approval. I felt like cheering too. At least one more car and one person were leaving.

Lots of people out there held bottles of beer or plastic cups—the cups we had put out. Obviously some of these kids—*many* of them—had been inside the house at one time. Thank goodness for Mike and Mo. They were keeping the crowd under some control. If all of those people had tried to come in, the house would have imploded or collapsed under the crush.

I'd been so busy and worried about what had been happening inside that I hadn't thought about looking outside. What were the neighbors thinking? They couldn't miss this. They had to be standing in their houses looking out their windows.

This wasn't good. My parents didn't really know any of the neighbors, but they did talk to them sometimes. Somebody was bound to mention this to them. Unless I mentioned it first. I could tell them there was some sort of big gathering on the street, some sort of party, but I didn't know where it had been held. It had to be at one of the neighbors' houses. Sometimes the best defense was a good offense.

Regardless, I couldn't hope to control what was happening out there, and at least it was happening out there instead of in here.

As I watched, a fight broke out between two guys. They started pushing and shoving. A punch was thrown and the crowd surged forward, surrounding and then separating them.

Then a second fight broke out and somebody smashed a bottle against the sidewalk. A car alarm went on, the car's horn honking and its lights flashing.

The whole thing was like a scene from a movie. I was glad to be inside.

"It's getting crazy out there," Jen said.

"Totally, but there's nothing we can do about it...is there?"

Jen shook her head. "Those people out there aren't at the party. We have no responsibility for them."

"But they wouldn't be out there if it wasn't for us having a party in here."

"*In* is the key word. What happens out there has nothing to do with us."

I thought she was wrong, but I really, really wanted to believe her.

"I guess you're right."

"Let's just keep taking care of things inside," she said.

"Of course. Why aren't you on the stairs?"

"Don't worry. I asked a couple of the guys to watch the stairs. They're taking care of it. Nobody is going to go upstairs. And more people are leaving all the time. Look."

Mike had the front door open and was letting out a couple of people. Two more down and another hundred to go. It was all starting to look like it just might work. Suddenly four guys pushed themselves in the door. Mike tried to stop them, but they were bigger and outnumbered him and Mo. Behind them came two girls and another guy.

Jen and I rushed to the door, getting there in time to help Mo slam the door shut and stop the flood.

Somebody started pounding on the door, and there was yelling and screaming from the people who had been kept out. They were angry, but I didn't care—they were outside and they weren't coming in no matter how hard they pounded.

That is, they weren't coming in until we tried to let somebody else out. What would happen then? We just had to hope that those people on the outside would get tired and go away before that happened.

There was a tremendous smash and people started to scream. It was coming from upstairs in the living room. I rushed up the stairs and stopped, stunned, unable to believe the scene. The entire floor was covered with broken glass. The big front picture window had been smashed. There was a gigantic hole in the window and there was a brick lying in the middle of the floor.

A girl was holding onto her arm, which was bleeding badly. It looked like she'd been cut by flying glass. She was crying and two other girls were holding onto her, trying to comfort her, but they weren't stopping the blood from dripping down onto the carpet.

Then a second brick smashed through the window, taking out part of the remaining glass, sending shards showering into the room. People screamed and yelled and pushed and shoved as they scrambled out of the way, bumping into each other, dropping their drinks and knocking over chairs.

I pressed against the wall as they rushed past and toward the door. Mike saw them coming and swung open the door. The mass of people tried to rush out, and at the same time some others on the outside saw an opportunity and tried to run in. There was a crash of bodies, people pushing and shoving and fighting to get past each other. Kids were jostled and trampled as bodies bounced against the wall and each other, but finally the force of the people trying to get out overpowered the others, and kids literally fell out through the door.

There was a loud smash and the music

just stopped. I turned back around in time to see my father's stereo fly through the air and out the picture window, taking one of the few pieces of glass still clinging to the frame.

There was more screaming and yelling, and then there was a tremendous smash of broken glass coming from the kitchen. More people ran out of the kitchen as I tried to force my way upstream to find out what had happened. I barged through the crowd and saw that the punch bowl was in a million pieces and the reddish fruit punch had stained the floor!

My mother's punch bowl—her antique family heirloom—was gone. How would I explain what had happened? I couldn't. I couldn't explain that or the broken windows.

I felt like crying. I wanted to just slump to the punch-stained floor, roll into a ball and cry. Instead I started to yell.

"Everybody get out! Everybody get out of my house!" I screamed at the top of my lungs.

The people in the kitchen stopped laughing and looked at me as if I were crazy. I *was* crazy.

"Get out of my house!" I screamed again. "I don't even know any of you! Get out!"

They stood there stunned. Nobody moved.

I reached over and slapped the drink out of a girl's hand. The plastic cup bounced against the wall and splattered onto the floor as she jumped backward.

"Get out of my house!" I screamed.

Everybody unfroze. Some of the people put down their drinks, and others just started moving out of the kitchen. Out of the kitchen was good. Now I wanted them out of my house.

I followed them into the living room and was met by a mass of people. My sudden burst of courage seemed to deflate. How could I ever get this many people to leave?

Just then I heard the sirens.

Chapter Ten

For the first few seconds I thought I was the only one who heard the sirens. Then, all at once, it was like everybody heard them. They stopped and listened. The sound was unmistakable and it was coming in this direction. The noise was getting louder and louder. Suddenly one kid moved toward the door, and then another and another, until everybody started running toward the front door.

There was a mass rush. It was like a school fire drill that had gone completely out of control. Drinks were dropped or tossed against the walls. Bodies began bouncing against each other as everybody tried to make it out of the house.

The front door was wide open—Mo and Mike were nowhere to be seen—and people streamed through, running outside.

I ran over to the front window, glass crunching under my feet and into the carpet.

The scene outside was wild. Hundreds of kids were on the run. It was like a wave of people. Some of them were running down the street, while others were heading out the other way, into the field at the end of the street. Others were jumping into cars. Vehicles were starting up, revving and trying to jockey away but were blocked by other cars trying to do the same thing.

One of the cars bounced up over the sidewalk and drove on the lawns of the neighbors! The driver bypassed the line of cars and then bumped back onto the road and into the intersection, squealing away.

The sirens—and it was clearly more than one siren—were getting louder. I didn't know if they were coming to my house or not. I was just grateful they were in the area. Maybe there was a fire or an emergency they were rushing to nearby. If that was the case, I had to get to the front door and lock it so that the people who had run out wouldn't come back once the sirens had passed.

Then the flashing lights appeared at the top of the street. It was a police car—no, *two* police cars. Then a third and a fourth and a fifth car appeared. They came up the street, blocking any other cars from leaving.

The cars were trapped, but the people on foot weren't. They turned around and started running toward the field and away from the police.

While the police had blocked the cars from leaving, they themselves were blocked from coming any closer. The doors of the stopped police cars opened and the officers got out—two per car.

The police fanned out across the width of the street. It was eerie watching them come toward us, their passage illuminated by the pulsing of the lights on their cars, radiating out and across the whole scene.

Jen appeared at my side. "I...I can't believe all of this. How did it happen?"

I shook my head. "I don't know. It just kept building and building until it was out of control."

"What are you going to say to the police?" she asked.

I hadn't even considered that. I was just so grateful that they'd appeared. I hadn't thought that they were going to come to the house. And it wasn't what I was going to say that was important, but what they were going to say to me. Even worse, what were they going to do to me? Was I going to be arrested?

The police officers started moving to the cars that lined the street. Doors were opened and drivers and passengers removed. Other cops formed a line on the street, forcing the remaining kids to run in the other direction. It didn't look like they were even trying to catch anybody, just moving them away to break things up. Most of the crowd had left, and most of those who remained were fleeing as fast as their legs could carry them. The only ones who couldn't run were Jen and me.

Then I looked down at the lawn. There was somebody lying there, not moving. How could somebody sleep through all of this? Maybe they weren't sleeping. They must have passed out.

"We have to get rid of all the alcohol," Jen said.

"What?" I asked. I understood the words but didn't know what she meant.

"We have to dump all the alcohol. We have to get rid of the bottles. We have to hide the evidence before the police get here!"

"Jen," I said, shaking my head, "it's over…there's nothing we can do…we can't hide all of this."

I gestured around the room. If only it was just the beer bottles that littered the room. There was the smashed-out front window, the pieces of glass in the carpets, broken bottles, garbage, overturned chairs, spilled drinks and stains on the carpets.

"There's nothing that can be done. Nothing."

I started to cry, and Jen put her arm around my shoulders.

"I'm so sorry," she said.

"So am I. But not as sorry as I know I'm going to be later."

Chapter Eleven

I watched as the ambulance slowly drove away, lights flashing. It was carrying the girl who passed out on the lawn. That was all it was. She had drunk so much that she passed out, and when the police arrived, her friends just ran off and left her. Nice friends.

The only vehicles left on the street were the police cars. The only people left in the house were Jen and me and the police. The officers strolled through the house, their big thick black boots grinding the glass and garbage even farther into the carpet. They'd been walking around, checking out the house, making sure nobody else was hiding or passed out. Occasionally I heard one or other of them comment that they were glad it wasn't their house.

A female officer came up to us.

"Here," she said, handing me a glass.

"Thanks," I said as I took it and had a small sip. It was water.

"How are you feeling?" she asked.

She had been nothing but nice to me. I'm not sure what I had expected, but they'd all been nice.

"I don't know how I feel," I said. "I guess just numb. I can't believe any of this happened. I can't believe it happened."

"I've seen worse," she said.

"Worse than this?" I gasped.

"Far worse. I've been to places where sinks have been smashed, toilets ripped out, walls broken, televisions stolen—"

"I stopped somebody from taking my father's digital camera," I said.

"You won't know what was taken until you and your parents check out the whole house. I wouldn't be surprised if lots of things have been stolen."

What an awful thought.

"And we can all be grateful that nobody was seriously hurt," the officer said. "There have been some real tragedies at parties like these. Broken bones, head injuries...there have even been deaths."

"Deaths?" I said.

"If you have hundreds of teenagers fueled by alcohol, with nobody to put on the brakes, there's no limit to how bad things can get."

I thought about that girl who had been cut by the flying glass. I wondered where she went, how badly she had been hurt and what would have happened if that brick had hit her in the head or if the glass had flown up into her eyes.

"Is that girl in the ambulance going to be okay?" Jen asked.

"She'll be fine. Alcohol poisoning. I talked to her. Stupid kid had never drunk before in her whole life, and tonight she chooses to down a whole mickey of whiskey."

The officer made a face like she was disgusted, and my stomach did a flip. The alcohol in that punch was more than I'd ever had before. I could only imagine how Jen was feeling.

"She'll be treated and released, probably tomorrow morning," the officer said. "I don't know what will be worse—the way her head is going to be feeling or facing her parents. And speaking of facing parents, we haven't been able to get in touch with your parents. Nobody is picking up at your grandmother's house."

"The phone is in my nana's room and she's hard of hearing. If she took out her hearing aid, she probably can't hear it ringing. She must be sleeping through it," I said. "What about my father's cell phone?"

"Nobody is picking up—it says the customer is not currently available."

"I guess my father turned his cell phone off."

"Were you able to get in touch with my mother?" Jen asked.

"She should be here soon," the officer said.

"Did she say anything?" Jen asked.

"What do you think?"

I had a pretty good idea. I wanted somebody here, but I was afraid of what Jen's mother would say, or what she'd think, and what she'd do. There was no telling how much trouble we were going to be in.

"It wasn't supposed to be like this," I said. "We just invited a few people."

"That's how it usually starts," the officer said. "A small gathering with a few people."

"Honestly, that's all we invited. We didn't even know most of those people. You have to believe us!" I pleaded.

"I do believe you. What happens is you invite somebody who mentions it to somebody else on their MSN, or they send

93

out an instant message, or some people make a few phone calls, and it just keeps building and building until it gets out of control and it can't be stopped."

"That's what happened. We tried to control it but we couldn't." I started crying again. I'd been crying on and off the whole time.

The officer put a hand on my shoulder. "It's over and there's nothing you can do. What we have to do is look at what will happen next. We can't just leave you here by yourself. We need to be able to leave you and the house in the hands of a responsible adult."

"How about my mother?" Jen asked. "Could she be in charge?"

"We could ask her when she gets here," the officer said.

"Do you think she'll agree?" I asked.

"I don't know what to expect," Jen said. "I can't even predict how she's going to react."

I knew we wouldn't have long to wait.

"You two seem like nice kids," the officer said.

"We are," Jen said. "I've never been in trouble in my life."

"Me neither."

"We all make mistakes," the officer said. "This one was a bad one, and hopefully you'll learn from it."

We heard a sound at the front door and another police officer walked in, followed by Jen's mother.

"My goodness, this is beyond belief," she said. She looked slowly around the room, taking in the whole scene.

"How could this happen?" she gasped.

There was no answer I could give.

"It looks awful," the officer said, "but it's only property damage. Nobody got hurt. That's the important thing."

Jen started to cry, and her mother rushed over and wrapped one arm around Jen and her other arm around me.

The last of the police drove away, leaving the three of us at the door. Jen's mother had agreed to take charge of us and the house. She had already called the number the police had given for the emergency glass-repair company. They were coming to replace the two smashed windows.

"Tomorrow you're going to have to explain this to your parents," she said to me.

"I know."

"But tonight we're all going to work," she said. "When you face your parents, it will be better if some of this is fixed."

"Thank you for understanding."

"To tell you the truth, I really don't understand how any of this could happen."

"Neither do we, and we were here," I said.

"The police officer called it the weekend plague," Jen's mother said. "She said it's happening more and more often, parties getting out of control."

"It was like a fire getting bigger and bigger," I said, trying to explain it.

She shook her head slowly, sadly. "We better check out the whole house."

I didn't want to go. I didn't want to see. I just wanted to go up to my room, climb into bed, pull the covers over my head and pretend that none of this was real. I couldn't do that.

We trailed behind her as she walked from room to room, surveying the scene. There was more damage than I'd remembered. There were stains and spilled drinks everywhere, puddles of vomit, broken furniture and holes in the wall where people had punched or kicked or tossed things. Phones had been ripped out of the wall, and a light had been torn right off the ceiling. The dinner plates had been smashed against a wall in the rec room and were in a million pieces on the floor. Some had been thrown so hard that they were embedded in the wall. The television set downstairs had been knocked over. We picked it up and turned it back on—luckily it still worked.

Upstairs it was obvious that somebody had been going through my parents' dresser drawers. Every drawer was open, and clothing had been thrown on the ground. Things had been taken, I was sure, but we wouldn't know what until my parents got home.

Spills could be mopped up and stains could be cleaned, but how could the other damage be fixed? And I didn't just mean the holes and the broken glass. How could I ever face my parents again? How could I fix the trust that had been broken?

I felt like curling up in a little ball and crying. It was all so overwhelming.

"I'm going to call your aunt and ask her to come and help," Jen's mother said. "An extra set of hands would be helpful. In the meantime, you two start with the kitchen. Clear the counters and then work your way down to the floor. We'll all work together, bit by bit. Let's get started."

"But the holes in the walls...the broken windows...the stereo on the lawn...I don't have the money to fix all of that."

I started to cry again and she put her arm around me.

"Your parents' insurance will cover some of the cost," she said. "And the rest will be split two ways."

"Two ways?"

"There were two people who were responsible." She turned to Jen. "Right?"

Jen nodded her head in agreement.

Chapter Twelve

I looked at my watch. It was almost two o'clock in the afternoon. Only a few more minutes until my parents were supposed to come home. The windows had been replaced and the garbage and bottles and even the stains on the carpet had been, for the most part, removed. If it weren't for the holes in the walls and the broken furniture, they might not have been able to tell that there had been a party.

Of course there was no way of hiding it or even trying to hide what had happened. There would be the bill for the glass replacement, and the comments from the neighbors, and the police coming over later today to meet with them.

Jen sat in the corner. She looked as tired and scared as I felt. This was going to be awful. Her mother was in the kitchen, still doing a few last-minute cleaning tasks. She had agreed to be here when my parents came home. She said that Jen needed to be here alongside me to take her share of the blame, and she'd be here to support both of us.

"That's it," Jen's mother said as she walked out of the kitchen, drying her hands on a dishcloth. "The place doesn't look too bad at all."

"Thanks for all your help," I said tiredly.

"It's the least we could do. Are you nervous?"

I shook my head. "Terrified. What do you think they're going to say?"

"I have a pretty good idea. They're going to yell and tell you how disappointed they are in you and wonder how you could ever let this happen and tell you how they don't know if they can ever leave you alone again or trust you." She paused. "And then they're going to hug you and thank God that you're all right, because it *is* going to be all right."

I heard the sound of a car pulling up to the house. I ran to the window. My father and mother climbed out of the car, carrying their small overnight bags. They looked happy to be home. That happiness wasn't going to last long.

"You better meet them at the front door," Jen's mother suggested.

I got up and went to the door, getting there just as they walked it.

"Mom...Dad. I'm so sorry. I have something I have to tell you."

Eric Walters began writing in 1993 as a way to entice his grade five students into becoming more interested in reading and writing. Since that first creation, Eric has published over forty-five novels. His novels have all become best-sellers, have won over thirty awards and have been translated into several languages.

Eric lives in Mississauga, Ontario, with his wife, Anita, and three children, Christina, Nicholas and Julia. When not writing, or playing and watching sports, he enjoys listening to jazz, playing his saxophone and eating in fine restaurants featuring drive-through service.

Orca Soundings

Orca Soundings

My Time as Caz Hazard
Tanya Lloyd Kyi

No More Pranks
Monique Polak

No Problem
Dayle Campbell Gaetz

One More Step
Sheree Fitch

Overdrive
Eric Walters

Refuge Cove
Lesley Choyce

Responsible
Darlene Ryan

Saving Grace
Darlene Ryan

Snitch
Norah McClintock

Something Girl
Beth Goobie

Sticks and Stones
Beth Goobie

Stuffed
Eric Walters

Tell
Norah McClintock

Thunderbowl
Lesley Choyce

Tough Trails
Irene Morck

The Trouble with Liberty
Kristin Butcher

Truth
Tanya Lloyd Kyi

Wave Warrior
Lesley Choyce

Who Owns Kelly Paddik?
Beth Goobie

Yellow Line
Sylvia Olsen

Zee's Way
Kristin Butcher

Visit www.orcabook.com for all Orca titles.